SIGNING
DAY

SIGNING DAY

K. R. COLEMAN

darbycreek
MINNEAPOLIS

Darby Creek
A division of Lerner Publishing Group, Inc.
241 First Avenue North
Minneapolis, MN 55401 USA

For reading levels and more information, look up this title at
www.lernerbooks.com.

The images in this book are used with the permission of: © pattern line/Shutterstock.com (scratch texture); © Eky Studio/Shutterstock.com (metal bolts); © Kriangsak Osvapoositkul/Shutterstock.com (rust texture); © Beto Chagas/Shutterstock.com (player walking away); © Betochagas13/Dreamstime.com (front player and stadium).

Main body text set in Janson Text LT Std 12/17.5.
Typeface provided by Adobe Systems.

Library of Congress Cataloging-in-Publication Data

Names: Coleman, K. R., author.
Title: Signing day / K.R. Coleman.
Description: Minneapolis : Darby Creek, [2017] | Series: Gridiron | Summary:When Iggy and his best friend, Malcolm, are offered football scholarships to rival schools, Iggy must decide whether to put family obligations before friendship.
Identifiers: LCCN 2016057703 (print) | LCCN 2017028162 (ebook) | ISBN 9781512448726 (eb pdf) | ISBN 9781512439830 (lb : alk. paper) | ISBN 9781512453553 (pb : alk. paper)
Subjects: | CYAC: Football—Fiction. | Friendship—Fiction. | College choice—Fiction. | Scholarships—Fiction. | High schools—Fiction. | Schools—Fiction.
Classification: LCC PZ7.1.C644 (ebook) | LCC PZ7.1.C644 Sig 2017 (print) | DDC [Fic]—dc23

LC record available at https://lccn.loc.gov/2016057703

Manufactured in the United States of America
2-44637-25781-7/21/2017

This book is dedicated to
Landon James Cole Mitchell.

Chapter 1

Coach calls for a time-out. There are just four minutes left on the clock. The North Shore Sharks are beating us by fourteen points. If we win, we go onto the state championship. If we lose, our season is over. Done. And it might be the last time I ever play.

It's my senior year, and I haven't gotten any offers to play college football. Last year I got some letters of interest, but college coaches didn't come knocking on my door. Time is running out. Playing at state is my last chance to get noticed. I'm determined to find a way to win this game.

"Iggy!" Calvin jogs over. We head across the field together. "We need to tie up this game."

"We need to do more than that," I say. "We need to win!"

"Then let's get it done," Calvin says. His face is serious and focused.

I know he feels the pressure too. He hasn't gotten any offers either, and he's a fantastic wide receiver—tall and fast with Velcro hands. But it's hard to get noticed when your school isn't known as a football powerhouse, and you live on an island 2,400 miles from the rest of the United States.

"It isn't over," Calvin says.

"Until the clock says zero," I finish, giving Calvin a somber smile. He's probably one of the few people who lives by that phrase—my dad's favorite phrase—as much as I do.

It's what my dad said after the doctor told him he had end-stage cancer and only a few months to live. He shook his head and said those words: It isn't over until the clock says zero. He proved that doctor wrong and lived another two years. But that was almost ten years ago.

"We need two more touchdowns," Calvin says with a smile. "How about I get one and you get the other?"

"Deal," I say as we jog over to Coach Kainoa. He's working furiously on his tablet and only looks up when we've all gathered around him.

"We need to throw them off," he says. "Do the unexpected."

I look over at Coach and then at Ty Gleason, our quarterback. "I have an idea," I say. "It's crazy, but it might work." Coach and Ty exchange a glance and nod at me to continue.

When I'm finished, Coach gives me another nod and says, "Let's do it."

He turns to me and grabs my helmet. Looking me straight in the eyes, he says, "You can't let the Sharks see what's coming. Don't look for Calvin until the last second."

I nod and we run back onto the field. When the ball is snapped, Ty laterals it to me.

The Sharks expect me to run the ball up the middle like I've done all game, but this time I cut left. I stop near the line of scrimmage and dig my back cleat into the turf. As soon as I spot Calvin wide open at the twenty yard line, I launch the ball high over the Sharks' heads. They turn and run, but it's too late—Calvin catches the ball, cradles it, and runs it in for a touchdown.

The crowd goes wild.

"Iggy!" Calvin yells to me over the roar of our fans as we head off the field. "You should be playing quarterback!"

"Nah." I shake off the suggestion. "Then I wouldn't get to run as much." And that's what I love most—getting the ball, blasting through a line of players and into the open, and running as hard and fast as I can. My father was a running back too. He played for Branford University. My mom says he could've gone pro if he hadn't joined the navy instead.

I turn around and glance at the clock. Two minutes and twelve seconds remain. A lot can happen in that time.

As Calvin and I approach the bench, Coach Kainoa's usually hard expression breaks into a grin and he shouts, "Flawless! We're in striking distance now! Keep it up!"

He's excited. We're all excited. I can feel the energy not only on the bench but also in the stands. The Regent Warriors have never made it to state. This is the first time in over twenty years we made it to the state semifinals.

Coach sends Louie, our kicker, onto the field for the extra point. Calvin and I stand together on the sidelines and watch the special teams head out. Louie is one of the smallest guys out on the field—only a sophomore and new to our school—but he's had a pretty good season.

The Sharks send out one of their best players—Rain Bok. The guy is huge and tough. He's an all-around player, taking the field for offense, defense, and even special teams, but his main role is running back. I've heard Rain is being recruited by a bunch of Big Ten colleges. He's a hot name among college coaches.

The Sharks' coach has connections from his early years coaching college ball and has contacted some old friends still in the business. Word has it that it's gone to Rain's head, and he's a pain to play with now that he's gotten all the attention.

In a loud, rumbling voice, Rain yells something at Louie to try and rattle him. It seems to work. I see Louie lose his focus and yell something back.

A whistle blasts. Everyone on the field lines up.

Just let it be good, let it be good, I think as Louie takes three stiff steps, but before the ball even leaves his foot, I know it won't be good.

The ball doesn't get the height it needs and Rain leaps into the air and blocks it. The ball falls to the ground.

Louie's shoulders crumple as the Sharks' fans cheer.

Chapter 2

There are less than two minutes left on the clock.

"We don't stop," Coach says, gathering us around before we take the field again. "We don't give up. We get the ball back and march it down the field. We score again." He looks over at Louie. "We need an onside kick. Just pop the ball ten yards—get some air under it and angle it to the left. We need to gain possession again."

Louie looks hesitant, like Rain's block is still getting to him.

"We need you back in the game," Coach

says to Louie. "We need you to do this." He turns to look at me and Calvin. "I'm sending you two out there. Your job is to recover the ball. Get it and run. Run as far and as fast as you can. And whatever you do, keep going. Every second counts. Got it?"

Calvin and I both nod at this. We jog onto the field with Louie and the rest of special teams.

The Sharks look fierce. I can see by the way they're positioned that they're ready to attack.

Louie's kick is perfect. Magical. It drops down only fifteen yards away. I run and get under it, scoop it up, and take off down the field.

Calvin is in front of me, shoulders down, channeling an inner-fullback I didn't know he had. He takes down a North Shore player, and I run around them, up the middle as fast as I can.

Two more North Shore players come after me, but I stiff arm one of them, spin out of the way, and run to the sideline. Heart beating, legs burning, I don't stop. Balancing along the green grass next to the white line, I move down the field. No one is in front of me. I make it to the Sharks' forty yard line, then the thirty. Out of the corner of my eye I see Rain Bok coming after me. I step out of bounds, but Rain hits me anyway. I fly through the air and land hard on the ground. It was a cheap hit—a late hit. But I'm not going to let it get to me.

Shake it off, I think. *Stay focused.*

"Just give up now," Rain yells at me as I cross the field, trying not to show him I felt that hit. I'm sure I'll have a bruised rib, but I walk upright and don't let him know I'm in any pain. "There's no way you and your loser team can win."

"It isn't over," I say with a nod to the scoreboard. "We still have time."

"It's over," he says, getting in my face.

Suddenly Calvin steps between us.

"Don't waste a second on him," he says. "Stay focused. Let's go."

We line up again.

The plan is for Calvin to get open in the end zone, and for Ty to throw him a pass. But the Sharks swarm as soon as the ball is snapped. They're all over Calvin and rush to take Ty down.

Ty doesn't have time to throw to Calvin, so he tosses the ball to me. I'm not ready for it and barely catch it in my fingertips.

There is a wall of players in front of me. I tuck the ball under my arm, put my shoulder down, and plow through the defense. Arms and bodies try to bring me down, but I twist and turn and keep going.

Touchdown!

We don't celebrate. We just need a two-point conversion to tie the game. There are five seconds left on the clock. I look at Calvin, and he looks at me.

This is it.

The ball is snapped.

Ty catches it.

The Sharks descend.

Four.

Three.

"Throw it," I yell.

Calvin is open.

Two.

Ty takes a step and throws it.

One.

Rain Bok picks it out of the air.

The game is over. Our season is done.

Chapter 3

The locker room is quiet. We've lost games before, but this loss is different. We all played our hearts out. We all thought we had a chance of making it to the state championship this year.

I notice Louie sitting on a bench, head down. I hit Calvin on the arm and nod to Louie. The two of us get up and head over to him. I sit on his left and Calvin sits on his right. Louie looks at us as if we're about to beat him up or something.

"I lost the game. I messed everything up," Louie says.

"Hey, it happens," I say, looking at him. "Sometimes things get messed up. We've all been there."

Louie doesn't seem to buy it.

"When I was a sophomore . . ." I say, looking at Calvin, who starts to smile. He knows the story I'm about to tell. "I ran the ball the wrong way down the field."

"He got hit by two defenders." Calvin takes over the story. "Got spun around, but managed to stay on his feet and hold onto the ball so he kept running—just didn't realize he was going the wrong way."

"Calvin had to dive after me and grab me by the ankle to try to stop me," I say.

"And he shook me off," Calvin says, grinning wide now. "He kept going."

"Until I heard Coach yelling his head off from the sidelines to stop and turn around. When I realized I was going the wrong way, I made a sudden U-turn—"

"And ran into me," Calvin laughs. "Now that was a messed up play. We lost that game big time."

Louie gives a half smile at this.

"You've got next year to redeem yourself," I tell him. "You'll be okay."

I head back to my locker and pull off my jersey. The writing on the back is slightly faded: Jones, 27. My father wore that same number when he played for the Branford Bears in college. I told this to Coach Kainoa after I made the team three years ago, and he made sure the number was mine.

We shower, get dressed, and pack our bags. Coach lets all the seniors keep our jerseys, but our helmets go on a shelf. I place mine next to Calvin's and think how, more than anything, I'll miss the two of us playing together.

We've been through a lot, and Calvin is practically family. We've been friends since we lived across the street from each other on the base. Both our dads served as naval officers, so we got close pretty quick. Even after my dad died and we moved off base—a few years before Calvin's dad retired from the navy— Calvin was always there for me.

Last year, when my mom got an offer for

a great job in DC, she considered turning it down so that I could stay in Oahu for my senior year. But Calvin's parents agreed to take me in for the year, and it's only made us closer.

Coach Kainoa walks into our locker room and writes our final stats on a huge whiteboard that hangs by the door. Next, he gathers us around.

"Good game," he says. "Amazing plays. Every single one of you played with heart and determination out there. You made me proud. It was a great way to cap off the season. Now bring it in."

We all circle around him, hands in the middle.

Coach points to the locker room door and says, "When you step through that door, take what you've learned from the game, from your teammates, from your wins and your losses, and use it to guide you forward. Don't look back—look forward. And seniors, listen up, this isn't the end. It's a new beginning for all of you. There's so much more to do and see and be. Tomorrow we'll celebrate. Meet at the beach for a little end-of-season blowout. You boys can hang out on the beach, and I'll catch us some fish for dinner. You've had an amazing season, but there's more to life than football. There's ocean and sky and families and friends and food."

Coach turns to me.

"Iggy, take us on out."

"One, two, three!" I shout.

"Warriors don't give up!" my teammates yell.

The words echo in the room.

This is it, I think as I head to the door. Even after everything Coach has just said, it feels weird not to be playing next year. I've played football since I was six. It was something my dad and I loved, and it made me feel closer to him after he died.

As I step outside, I see my mom standing beneath a palm tree and I head over to her. I know she works very hard, and I can't ask her to do more, but I need to think about my future. I want to focus on getting into a good college, but I need to figure out a way to pay for it. My dad's illness drained my parents' savings, and we never really dug ourselves out of that hole. We were barely getting by before my mom got her new job.

My mom gives me a huge hug. She's flown all the way from DC for this game. I'm glad she could be here.

"You played strong out there," my mom whispers in my ear. "Your dad would be so proud of you. You didn't stop until the clock said zero."

I nod at this and try to imagine my dad standing here next to my mom, but as the years have passed, it has become harder and harder to picture him clearly. My mom brushes my bangs out of my eyes.

"I bought a ticket for you to come stay with me at Christmas," she says. "I'll show you around DC We'll talk about next year. Hang in there. Everything will work out."

We talk for a couple more minutes before Mrs. Gibson, Calvin's mom, pulls up to take my mom to the airport. She's taking a red-eye back to DC It was the cheapest flight she could find. "I've got to go," she says.

"Text me when you land," I say.

"I will." She gives me another quick hug and gets in the car.

Mrs. Gibson rolls down her window. "I'll meet you all at home. I'm going to pick up a pizza on my way back."

I watch them drive off before I head over to where Calvin and his dad are waiting.

"You two did everything you could out there," Mr. Gibson says. "Made some really great plays." He clicks the key fob to unlock the doors on his truck. Just as I reach for the door handle, a man approaches us.

"Ignatius Jones and Calvin Gibson?" the man says.

Calvin and I both turn. No one I know calls me Ignatius, not even my mom.

"I'm Calvin's father," Mr. Gibson says, stepping forward.

"I'm Wallace Henry," the man says. The name is familiar, but I can't place it right away.

Then it clicks. Wallace Henry. My dad and I used to watch him play football on TV.

Chapter 4

"**Y**ou used to play tight end," I say.

"Yes, I did," he says with a grin. "Can't believe you know that. I only played pro for two seasons before I screwed up my back."

"You played at UCC," I say. "My dad played against you at Branford. He knew who you were. I remember him pointing you out when you played."

"I'd love to talk to your dad. Where is he?"

This moment is never easy. I know it always makes people uncomfortable. When I tell Mr. Henry my dad is gone, he looks me in the eye and says, "I'm sorry—I hadn't heard."

After an awkward pause, he takes a silver case from his pocket and pulls out two business cards.

"I work for UCC as a recruiter now," he says. He smiles at me and adds, "I know, I know, Branford's biggest rival, but we're not that bad."

I smile too. When my dad and I would watch the Branford Bears play the UCC Titans, he never booed the Titans. He respected them as a team, even though he cheered like crazy for the Bears to beat them.

"So what's the deal? Are you recruiting these boys?" Mr. Gibson looks at Mr. Henry. What I've learned about Mr. Gibson in this past year is that he likes people to get to the point.

"I was here to watch another player, but these two boys caught my eye," Mr. Henry turns to Mr. Gibson. "I've watched a lot of high school games over the years, but this game had me on my feet. These two young men kept their team in the game. They showed a lot of promise out there. That is something we're looking for at UCC. Not only talent, but promise."

I look down at the card in my hand. Black

block letters against white. *Wallace J. Henry*, it says at the top. And then beneath his name are the words *University of Coastal California, Division I* in crimson.

"Why haven't we seen you two at camps before?" Mr. Henry asks.

"It's a long way to the mainland," Mr. Gibson says. "Those college football camps are expensive and not easy to get to when you live this far away."

Mr. Henry nods. "I looked up both of your stats," he says, taking out his phone and reading them off. "Calvin here has had 40 receptions for 476 yards and 16 touchdowns."

Calvin nods at this. Mr. Henry looks down at his phone and back at me. "You've got some pretty impressive numbers too: 310 carries for 2,211 yards and 15 touchdowns."

"Yes, sir," I say.

"Plans for next year?" Mr. Henry asks both of us.

Calvin and I look at each other.

"We'd like to play college football for a school like yours," Calvin says.

"Yes, sir," I add. "We want a chance to play."

Mr. Gibson says to Mr. Henry, "A school like UCC would be lucky to have these two. They're hard workers. I've never seen either one of them give up, and on top of all of that, they are smart, good kids."

"Well, I'd certainly like to be in touch," says Mr. Henry. He takes out another card, flips it over to the blank white side, and hands it to Calvin and me. "Write down your email addresses, would you?"

While we're doing that, he keeps talking. "I'd like you both to send me your game tapes and school transcripts." Mr. Henry points to the card in my hand. "And it might interest you to know that UCC and a couple of other schools in the area are holding a football camp in a few weeks. We like to call it the last-chance camp. It's an opportunity for seniors to show off their talent to coaches and staff still looking for players. I'd like to extend an invitation to both of you. I'll be there with the UCC coaches."

Mr Gibson still looked uncertain.

"Let me see what I can do about getting you two an official visit to our campus around the same time. We could help out with airfare and accommodations too."

Mr. Gibson nods at this.

"That would be great," I say.

"Thank you," Calvin says as he hands back the card we wrote on.

"And your coach, Freddie Kainoa, tell him to give me a call too," Wallace Henry says. "He was a great college player. I remember him from back in the day. I'd like to talk to him."

Calvin and I look at each other. We knew Coach played in high school, but he's never mentioned he played college football.

"I'll be in touch," Mr. Henry says.

We watch him head across the parking lot toward Rain Bok and his dad. Rain doesn't even look up at him. He continues to text on his phone. The kid probably has a dozen recruiters talking to him every day.

Chapter 5

When we get home, I grab my laptop and look up Wallace Henry. There he is—UCC's top recruiter.

"He's known for unearthing unknown talent," Calvin reads.

"That's us," I say. "Unknown."

"Not anymore," Calvin says.

I nod at this and open my email. As usual, Coach has already emailed us a recording of today's game. I click on the video, and Calvin and I watch the game as spectators instead of players.

Calvin opens his own laptop, and for the

next few minutes we sit side by side as we download footage, cut and copy our best plays, and add them to our game tapes. As we work, I ask, "Do you think we would've gotten more attention from recruiters if we'd played for a team like the Sharks?"

We've sent game tapes to dozens of schools, but we've never heard a word.

"I don't know if we would've gotten that much time on the field," Calvin says. "The Sharks have a lot of really good players. Maybe we would've been stuck on the bench."

"Maybe," I say.

Calvin finishes cutting together his last couple of clips, and I add our stats at the end.

"I'm glad we played for the Warriors," I say as I type a note of thanks to Mr. Henry. "It was a good time."

"It was," Calvin agrees, attaching a video file to his own email draft.

"Well," I say, looking over at Calvin, "I hope Mr. Henry was serious about giving us a shot."

We press send at the same time.

Chapter 6

The next day, I slather on sunscreen and put on a baseball cap.

Calvin laughs at me.

"You look like a tourist."

"No," I say. "I'd look like a tourist if I was burnt to a crisp."

When we get to the beach we see Coach pulling a boat into the dock. We wave and walk over.

"I've been out since early this morning," he calls to us. "Caught a couple of big ones! We're eating well tonight, boys."

Calvin and I smile and help Coach unload

supplies from the boat. As we carry his fishing gear and a few massive coolers of fish down the beach, we tell Coach about Mr. Henry approaching us in the parking lot.

"He wants you to call him," I say.

"He called me this morning," Coach says. "He wanted to know all about you two."

"What did you say?" I ask.

"That you two are strong and focused athletes. That you're coachable and natural leaders. That they'd be lucky to get you both."

"Do you think UCC is really interested?" I ask.

"They see you have talent and potential," he says. "They don't invite players to tour their program if they aren't serious."

By now some of the other players have shown up on the beach. We look out to the water where a couple of the guys are swimming. Ty grabs Louie from behind and tosses him into the crashing waves. For a second it looks like Louie won't come up, but then he reappears, spluttering and laughing. They splash water at each other and yell in surprise when another wave comes crashing in on them.

"Watch yourselves out there!" Coach yells as they bob to the surface again. "We need Louie in one piece for next season!"

The guys in the water laugh but come in closer to the beach all the same.

***

A little while later, Coach gathers us around and teaches us to clean the fish he's caught. After they're cleaned, we wrap the fish in palm leaves and cook them over hot coals on a grill. When they're done, we sit around on the sand, looking out over the water as we laugh and eat.

Eventually it gets dark. No one seems to want to leave, but one by one, guys start to head out. Calvin and I stick around and help haul things to Coach's truck.

"Make sure you follow up with Wallace Henry," he tells us. "Let him know that you want to play for UCC. Let him know you're willing to work hard for a place on the team."

"We want this," Calvin assures him. "To play Division I football would be incredible."

"Yeah, and you boys deserve it," Coach says with a grin. "You've worked so hard. But you'll have to keep working hard if you want to get on that team and stay on it. Understand?"

"Yes, Coach," Calvin and I say together.

"So you used to play college football?" Calvin says as we put the cooler in the back of Coach's truck.

Coach is silent for a minute.

"Mr. Henry mentioned it," I explain.

"I played for a season," he says. "I wish I would've played longer."

"What happened?" I ask.

"Spent too much time partying and not enough time studying," he says in a voice that's supposed to sound casual but doesn't. "I flunked out my second semester. It was bad. I lost my scholarship and ended my career."

Calvin and I stand there speechless. Coach has always seemed so focused.

"I made a mess," Coach says. "But I worked hard to clean it up. I got a job, went to a community college, got my grades up. After two years, the school let me back in, but I didn't get back on the team. I'm happy now. I moved on, but it would've been great to play a few more years."

He shuts the tailgate and looks at us.

"I'm rooting for you two. I know that you both have what it takes. But you're going to have to work for it. Training starts tomorrow morning at seven. Meet me on the field."

Chapter 7

The next day, Calvin and I head to the football field behind Regent High.

Coach is setting up cones when we arrive.

"Let's get going," he says. "We've got some work to do."

"Wallace Henry hasn't even emailed us back," Calvin says.

"Be patient," Coach replies. "But be prepared."

We follow him down to the end zone.

"Do you want an invitation to UCC?" Coach asks.

"Yeah," Calvin and I both say.

"Do want to play college football?"

"Yeah," we both say again.

"I didn't hear you," Coach says.

"Yes!" we both shout.

"Louder! Loud enough for the coaches at UCC to hear!" he yells again, pointing in the direction of the mainland.

"Yes!" we shout again.

"Then want it and work for it," he says. "You need to set yourself apart from the others. Win every drill. Stand out. Got it?"

Calvin and I nod.

Coach has Calvin and me line up on the white line at the end zone. He walks down to the forty yard line.

"Sprints," Coach says.

We get into position.

"Ready?" he yells. "Get set. Go!"

He blows his whistle.

Calvin and I race each other, arms and legs pumping. Calvin's long legs work furiously, but I stay right beside him and pass him at the very end.

"Let's do it again," Calvin says, panting hard but flashing a competitive smile my way.

"When you first start running, keep your chin down," Coach says. "If you stand up too fast, you limit your leg drive. Stay low."

We race again. Calvin wins this time, but I improve my time by a tenth of a second. We race again and again.

When we stop and drink some water, Coach looks at the two of us.

"Keep pushing each other," he says. "You've got this."

We work at all the drills, repeating them over and over.

At the end of the set, Coach tells us, "Come back here this evening. We'll run the drills again. And we'll run them every day after school. In the meantime, keep your body stretched and loose. Get sleep, stay hydrated. And remember, you've got one chance. A split second can make or break you. Push yourselves like you've never pushed yourselves before."

Chapter 8

That night, Wallace Henry calls Calvin while the two of us are studying in Calvin's room.

"It's Wallace Henry," Calvin says, covering the phone with his hand. I shut my book and move over to sit next to him.

"Yes," Calvin says and then, "Iggy's here too if you want me to put you on speaker phone."

There's a pause, and for a moment I think that he doesn't want to talk to me, just to Calvin, but then I hear Mr. Henry's voice.

"I watched your videos," Mr. Henry says.

Iggy and I both hold our breath and hover over the phone.

"Are you there?" he asks.

"Yes, sir," we say at the same time.

"I showed them to some people around here, and Coach Washington wants you both to come out for a visit. I've scheduled it for the last Friday of this month, the same weekend as the last-chance camp. That way, we pay for your plane tickets, and you get a tour, plus a chance to watch the Titans play against the Branford Bears on Saturday. On Sunday you'll have to take a bus to and from the camp to be sure we don't break any rules, but we'll take care of you once you're back on campus. For now, work hard and be ready. The coaches at the camp will be clocking your speed and testing your strength and endurance. Run all your basic drills. Know them blindfolded."

"Thank you," I say, trying to take it all in: an official visit, watching the Titans play the Bears, last-chance camp, drills, coaches. It's all happening so fast.

"I'll have someone here take care of your tickets, and I'll email you the details."

"We won't disappoint you," Calvin says.

Mr. Henry is silent a few moments then says, "Coach Washington makes the final decision. I just bring him the talent. There have been dozens of prospects who have visited the school already, and there are only a few more scholarships left. This isn't a sure thing."

"We understand," I say. "We're prepared to work hard. Can you tell us what Coach Washington is looking for?"

"Speed and strength," Mr. Henry says. "Practice as hard as you can to get things right."

After Mr. Henry ends the call, Calvin and I don't move right away. Then we both start yelling. No, not just yelling, roaring. Making so much noise that Calvin's parents both run into the room.

We tell them everything, and then I call my mom.

This starts to feel real for the first time. Calvin and I might have a future on the field— as teammates—after all.

Chapter 9

In what seems like no time, Mrs. Gibson is dropping us off at the airport for our trip to the mainland.

After we check in and head to our gate, we find out our plane is delayed. A mechanical problem, we're told.

"This isn't good," Calvin says, pacing back and forth in the waiting area. "What if they cancel our flight?"

"Then we get the next one out," I say. I try to stay calm, but I'm anxious too. We've spent so much time preparing for the trip. Using every spare minute we could find to watch

UCC game footage, lift weights, and run drills. Every moment we have on campus counts.

I get us some food, and we sit in uncomfortable plastic chairs and wait.

"We'll get there," I say, looking out the airport window at our plane. The sky is going dark. "We have to get there."

***

It's after midnight when our plane finally takes off. I try to get some sleep during the flight, but my mind won't turn off. I start thinking about all the things I want to do with my life—get a scholarship, play college football, graduate, work in medicine, find a better way to treat cancer—and I think about how this trip could be the start of my dreams.

It's a long time until I finally get sleepy. I close my eyes, but just when I start to drift off, the cabin lights go on, and we begin our descent.

My head feels fuzzy as we walk through the airport. Calvin and I duck into a bathroom where we change into dress clothes and splash water on our faces so that we look presentable. Then we grab our stuff and go to meet Mr. Henry outside the baggage claim area—except, he isn't there. We look around for him and then check our phones.

"Mr. Henry is in a meeting," Calvin says as he looks at his phone. "He said his assistant will pick us up. She'll be driving a red car."

Calvin and I hoist our bags over our shoulders and walk around outside. We see a woman with long, brown hair holding a sign with the words *Ignatius and Calvin.*

She smiles as we approach.

"Iggy," I say and shake her hand. "No one calls me Ignatius."

"It's quite a name," she says. "Kasey," she adds, introducing herself. "I'm Mr. Henry's intern."

She opens the trunk of the red convertible. Only one bag will fit. Calvin throws his bag in and then jumps in the front seat. I throw mine in the backseat and sit beside it.

"Nice car," Calvin says.

"It's Mr. Henry's," Kasey says as she buckles her seatbelt. "He meant to come get you himself, but he didn't think you'd be this late."

"We didn't either," Calvin says.

"Are you a student?" I lean forward and ask. She looks young.

"A senior," she says. "I'm working for Mr. Henry because I hope to get into college sports someday." She turns around and looks at me. "Buckle your seatbelt."

I quickly click the belt.

"Thanks for picking us up," Calvin says.

"No problem," Kasey replies as she exits onto a six-lane highway. "I'm hoping we can make good time. Mr. Henry wanted you two to be there for the team practice."

Calvin and Kasey keep talking up front, but the wind and the traffic make it too hard for me to hear anything, so I just sit in the back and try to fight off my exhaustion.

Pretty soon Kasey exits the highway, and after a few miles, I see the red brick buildings off in the distance. This must be the university. It's smaller than I imagined. I don't have a

40

lot of experience with college campuses, but
I expected something more like Branford
University. It's a beautiful campus. My dad
took me there for a game when I was eight. I
remember driving up this long road lined with
palm trees, and gold-colored foothills rising up
behind the campus.

"Here we are," Kasey says, pulling up next
to the athletic building. "We've missed the start
of practice by now. We should hurry. I'm sure
Mr. Henry wants to get you guys out there."

Chapter 10

With our bags slung over our shoulders, we follow Kasey into the athletic building and up to Mr. Henry's office. Kasey hands him back his keys and leaves.

Mr. Henry looks us up and down.

"Why don't you change into something a little more causal for practice. Grab your bags and follow me."

I'm suddenly nervous—why do we need to change? I thought we were just going to watch. I remember a rule about not playing with the team on official visits. My mind is racing.

Mr. Henry leads us outside and down to the field. He shows us to an empty locker room where we can change.

"The team just has a captain's practice today," Mr. Henry explains. "So there won't technically be any involvement from the coaches. Just think of it as a bunch of friends messing around. Get dressed—full pads—and meet me outside." And with that, Mr. Henry leaves the locker room.

This doesn't feel right to me.

"Do you think we'll get a chance to throw the ball around out there?" Calvin asks as we get dressed. He looks bright and alert.

"I don't know," I say. "But aren't we, uh—" I try to think of a way to say this without making it sound like an accusation. "Aren't we technically not supposed to be playing with the team?"

"It's not an official practice," Calvin replies. "You heard what Mr. Henry said. It's just a captain's practice. They're just getting loose. It's no big deal."

When we meet Mr. Henry outside the locker room, he hands us each an official UCC helmet. "See if they fit," he says.

We put them on and look at each other. The UCC logo is painted in crimson and gold on the sides.

"They look good on you," Mr. Henry says, and then we follow him out on the field.

"Big game tomorrow," he tells us. "Everyone's a little nervous. I'm not sure if they'll let you take the field, but if any of the guys wave you over, get out there, listen to what they say, and do something to impress them."

Now I'm really nervous. *So much for just a bunch of friends messing around*, I think.

We watch the team practice. They move through some plays. After a few minutes, the players break into different groups and scatter to the four corners of the field. One of the captains signals Calvin to head onto the field, and they include him in a passing drill.

I watch as Calvin gets in a line behind three other players. He's as tall as the guys on the team, but he looks skinny. When it's his turn, he runs and catches a pass. It's a beautiful catch. They have him run the drill five more times. Each time he catches the ball. Then they send him off the field.

"Velcro hands," I say with a grin when he's back standing next to me. "You looked good out there."

"Thanks," he says as he takes a sip of water. "I pretended that I was just playing with the Warriors back home."

I wait for someone to call me out on the field. I wait and wait, but no one says anything. And then the guys all huddle up and head to the locker room.

"Wait here," Mr. Henry says to me as he runs after one of the captains who was helping lead the practice.

A part of me hopes that no one asks me to do anything. I still feel a little uncomfortable with this whole thing. But another part of me wants to go out on that field and run and prove that I belong here.

The player Mr. Henry's talking to nods, disappears for a minute, and comes back with five players. The players look a little annoyed at being kept after practice.

"This is Iggy Jones," Mr. Henry introduces me to everyone.

"We're going to see what he can do," the captain says. "It's going to be him against the three of us." He points to two big guys and himself. "And you"—he points to three other guys—"are going to be his offensive line. He's going to run the ball. Defense is going to try and stop him with a two-hand touch." He looks at the players. "No tackling the prospect. Got it?"

They all nod, except one guy who just gives a soft laugh.

The captain looks at me. "I don't trust them not to tackle you, so run fast."

We line up on the field. Three guys on defense. Three guys in front of me on offense.

I put my chin down and stare straight ahead.

The ball is tossed to me.

This is it, I think.

The three offensive linemen cover me for a few seconds, and I run behind the biggest one as he blocks, but he doesn't seem to be trying too hard. One of the guys playing defense breaks through. I cut right, get around him and move down the field. Another defender chases after me. I can feel him just behind, so I run faster, pumping my legs and arms hard. I can hear my heart beating in my head. Just before I get to the end zone, I feel two hands on my back, and then a shove. I fly forward and somersault across the ground. When I look up, I see three players staring down at me.

"You're fast," one of the players laughs as he reaches his hand down to me and helps me up.

"Almost made it," I say with a smile.

"Almost doesn't get you points up on the board," the captain says with a shake of his head. Then he looks up at the stands. It isn't until then that I realize Coach Washington is standing in the bleachers with a couple of his assistant coaches.

Calvin walks over and hands me a bottle of water.

"You looked good out there," he says. "Fast."

"Until the somersault at the end," I say, trying not to make eye contact with the coaches.

"You!" a voice booms. We look up. Coach Washington is pointing over at us. "On the field. Now." I'm not sure who he's talking to.

"Mr. Jones," he points to me.

Another player grabs me and takes me out on the field. I realize it's the starting quarterback.

"Throw the ball," Coach Washington orders me. Then he points at Calvin. "You, get out there and catch the ball."

Calvin jogs out on the field too.

For a good fifteen minutes, I throw the ball to Calvin. He catches it every time.

"Thank you," Coach Washington says, still standing in the bleachers. Then he turns around and walks away.

I look over at the quarterback, who didn't do anything but stand there the whole time.

"What was that about?" I ask as Calvin jogs over.

"He's been searching for a new quarterback," he says. "I graduate this spring."

I blink. "I'm not a quarterback."

"Coach Washington can make you into anything he wants you to be." The guy heads back to the locker room.

"I've always thought you should be playing quarterback," Calvin says to me. "Imagine you and me out there. You throwing. Me catching. We'd be invincible."

But I'm not so sure.

Chapter 11

We pass the UCC locker room as we head back to change. I can hear the guys goofing around. Singing. Shouting. Getting psyched for the big game against the Bears tomorrow.

Calvin and I head into the locker room down the hall. It's just the two of us in there.

"Well," Calvin says, sounding optimistic. "We made it on the field."

"We did," I say.

I don't feel as sure as Calvin sounds like he is. It makes me nervous that the coaches had really been watching the whole time. Like we were doing something wrong.

"Now we just have to stand out on Sunday. Show them that we're serious."

Mr. Henry is waiting for us outside the locker room.

"You both looked good out there," he says. "But I'm going to be honest with you, Coach Washington has his eyes on two other recruits. I think you made an impression, but you're going to have to shine on Sunday. Prove that you have what it takes. You aren't there yet."

"I got taken down," I say.

"Yes, you did," Mr. Henry says. "But that guy is the fastest running back in the league. Legs, they call him."

"What year is he?" I ask

"A freshman," Mr. Henry replies casually.

I nod at this. I don't know how much playing time I'd get if I'm up against a guy named Legs.

Mr. Henry seems to know what I'm thinking. "You were fast," he says to me, "but not fast enough."

I feel as if there is a stone in my throat. It's making it very hard to swallow.

"But don't worry," Mr. Henry continues. "We all like how you throw. The problem with guys who've played quarterback all through high school is they've already developed bad habits and stubbornly try to keep them. But you've got great accuracy and can learn from the best. You and Calvin out there together make a good team."

But I'm a running back, I think. *That's what I love.*

Chapter 12

Kasey meats us outside the athletic building and walks us to a nearby dorm where she introduces us to the guys we'll be staying with.

"This is Shawntrell," she says. I recognize Shawntrell as one of the guys out on the field with me. *At least he isn't Legs*, I think. But then . . . "And this is Oscar," she says. "But everyone calls him Legs."

I look at him, but he doesn't seem to see me standing there. He looks past me. I turn around to see what he's looking at, but there's nothing behind me. He just doesn't want to acknowledge that I'm there.

Kasey hands us each a plastic card. "These will get you into the cafeteria. Each card has $200 on it. That should be enough to keep you fed this weekend, but with football players, I'm never sure."

"It's good," I say. "Thanks!"

"After you eat," Kasey continues, "I'll meet you both again right here, and we'll walk around campus. Then I'm going to take you to a class or two so you can see what academic life is like here."

We both thank her again.

"Enjoy!" She smiles. "I'll meet you back here in forty-five minutes."

We head upstairs to the dorm rooms we'll be sharing with Shawntrell and Legs.

"Let me stay with Shawntrell," I whisper to Calvin. "I'm pretty sure Legs would like to smother me in my sleep. I'd be his competition if I went here next year."

Calvin nods at this. "Weird that they put you two together."

"It is," I agree.

I put my stuff in Shawntrell's room. There's

an extra cot set up there for me. Calvin is just across the hall in Legs' room. The entire football team is housed in this building. The coach doesn't let his players live off campus. He keeps them all together so they can help each other out.

"Let's get our second breakfast," Shawntrell says.

"Second?" I say.

"We eat before practice and after," Shawntrell says. "Trying to put on some weight." He looks at Calvin. "You, kid, need like four breakfasts."

We follow Legs and Shawntrell across a courtyard.

"So, you're from Hawaii," Legs says, finally speaking to us. "Why would you ever leave?"

"A chance to play here," Calvin says. "Where are you from?"

"Texas," he answers.

"Chicago," Shawntrell adds.

We keep talking about UCC and classes as we make our way through the cafeteria, and Legs seems to be warming up to me.

But then he gives Shawntrell a nod and joins some other players a few tables over.

"Don't take it personally," Shawntrell says to me. "Coach has been riding him hard. I think he made sure you two were paired up to light a little fire under him. Legs has got natural talent, but he needs to work harder."

I don't like that I'm here just to threaten another player. It doesn't feel good.

Some other freshman players join us, and they all start talking about Saturday's game. Shawntrell is worried about beating Branford. UCC isn't as strong as they were the year before. They lost some of their top players. I don't mention that my dad went to Branford.

"How much playing time do you get?" I ask.

"None," Shawntrell says. "But Legs, over there, he's been sent out quite a bit. Hopefully next year I'll get out on the field. You have to work hard, prove yourself, and fight for a spot on the field your sophomore year. But you never know."

We clear our trays and head back to the dorm.

Legs walks past us without saying a word. I watch him move up ahead. His strides are long and confident. His head is held high.

I need to prove that I'm the fastest guy out there on Sunday, I think. Not second fastest. Not third fastest. *The* fastest. Coach Washington is looking for speed.

Chapter 13

I want to head back to a field and work on my sprinting, but there's no time. Kasey is waiting to take us to some classes and give us a tour of the campus. We spend the day in a whirlwind of activity.

Just before dinner we head back to Mr. Henry's office, and he introduces us to a bunch of staff. I'm exhausted, but I pretend to be wide awake, alert, interested in everything everyone has to say. I want to make a good impression. This is my shot, and I don't want to screw it up. After a lot of hand shaking and too many names for me to ever remember, we're swept out of the room and Kasey picks us up again.

When we finally get back to the dorms, there isn't time to relax. After an early dinner, we walk with the entire team to the athletic building. Coach Washington is waiting outside. He leads the team to a glass case where he takes out a large golden bell.

My dad once told me about how UCC beat his team the first year he played at Branford and how they took back the Golden State Bell. He was determined to beat the UCC Titans the next year and get the Golden State Bell back, but Branford lost again. It took his team three years to finally win it back.

Coach Washington takes the bell off the stand and rings it five times.

"The Golden State Bell has been ours for five years!" Coach says with pride. "Tomorrow we play to keep it. So what are we going to do tomorrow?"

"Beat the Bears!" the team shouts.

He rings the bell one more time.

There's so much excitement in the air. A current of energy. But I don't feel as if I'm a part of it. I'm not heading out on the field. I'll be watching from the stands—where I know I'll quietly cheer for my father's team because I remember so many Saturdays watching the Branford Bears play football on TV.

Chapter

14

We head back to the dorm. Lights out for
the team is at ten, but the rest of campus is
wide awake. There is yelling and singing.
At one point I even hear what sounds like a
marching band coming down the street, but
I'm so tired, I fall asleep to the beat of a drum
and the sound of a tuba playing just outside
the window.

The next morning we wake up early and
have breakfast with the team, but then they go
off to get ready for the game. Kasey meets us
back at the dorms and hands us UCC T-shirts
and hats, then gives us some time alone.

We're supposed to meet Mr. Henry outside the stadium, but not until noon. So Calvin and I head out to a patch of lawn between dorm buildings. We stretch and sprint, then run through some drills. It feels good to be outside running around.

After we're done, we both lie on the grass and look up at the blue California sky above us.

"I want this," Calvin says. "More than anything, I want to go here. I want to be a part of this team."

We lay there silently, and I think about what I pictured for myself—for college and my future. I wonder if my picture is the same as Calvin's.

***

The campus is filled with people dressed in blue and silver and red and gold. Music is playing. Grills are smoking. The energy of game day distracts me from all my doubts.

We walk around and take in all the activity until we meet up with Mr. Henry at noon. He leads us into the stadium and down to our seats. We're right behind the UCC bench. When the guys come out on the field, we're so close that Shawntrell gives us a high-five. He's suited up, but not expected to play.

The band plays. The crowd cheers. The Titans and the Bears have an intense game. At halftime, the score is tied 21–21, but during the second half, the Bears march down the field and score two touchdowns. By the fourth quarter the score is 35–21, and to add insult to injury, the Branford Bears end up getting another touchdown with just seconds left in the game.

I'm happy the Bears won, but there's no one to celebrate it with.

"Don't you dare smile," Calvin warns me. "Look disappointed."

So I just pull my new UCC cap lower on my head to shade my face.

As we head out of the stadium, Calvin makes a good point. "I wonder if the coaches will be in a bad mood tomorrow," he says. "It would've been better for us if the Titans had won."

"Good point," I say as we walk past Branford fans celebrating with each other.

We know our roommates won't be in a great mood, so Calvin and I decide to give them some space. We wander around campus and the surrounding neighborhood for the rest of the evening, not heading back to the dorms until ten. Shawntrell is already sleeping when I get back, and I know I should get some sleep too, but I can't stop thinking about all I have to do the next day.

Chapter 15

Sunday morning, Calvin and I are both up at 6:00 a.m. We grab our gear, get some breakfast, and head outside to wait for the city bus that will take us to the last-chance camp. The morning air is damp and cool.

Calvin seems energized. He looks at me and says, "Let's do this. You and me. Let's dominate today!"

We get on the bus, and I feel like I might be more awake than I have ever been in my entire life. This morning I have a chance to prove that I've got what it takes to play college football, and I'm determined to make the most of it.

When we get to the camp, we see groups of coaches and assistant coaches standing around on the field. I can't tell who is from where because we're so far away.

We're taken to the locker room where there are at least forty other guys scrambling for a place to change, and I know there are even more guys in the locker room next door.

Calvin glances around and starts to look nervous. "There are a lot of guys trying out," he says.

"A lot more than I thought," I agree.

I unzip my bag and change into my gear. As I walk to a fountain to fill up my water bottle, I hear someone say that a coach from Branford is here. I can't help but think of my dad. I imagine him doing everything he could to introduce me to the Branford coaches and staff. I know he would've wanted me to play for them, but no one there knows me, and my dad isn't around to make any phone calls for me.

When we get out on the field, I'm given a white practice jersey, and Calvin is given a yellow one. Our last names and a number are written across tape on the back. Calvin and I are directed to different stations set up on the field.

"Good luck," I say.

"You too," Calvin says, and we turn and walk in different directions.

My first station is the forty-yard dash. We don't race alone. I'm paired with a tall guy, and we stand at the end of the line.

When it's my turn, I get into position. The player I'm about to race against says something to me, but I don't hear his words. I'm in the zone. Focused on what I need to do.

The whistle blows. I take off, chin down, running as fast as I can. I don't even feel my feet hit the ground. I cross the finish line first. It's my fastest time yet.

I'm paired with a new partner, and I get a chance to run again. I'm feeling good, getting into the groove, and gaining confidence.

We head to the next station. It's the three-cone drill. When it's my turn, I stumble as I round the second cone. I look down and see that my cleat came untied.

"I'd like to run it again," I say, pointing to my shoe.

The guy with the stopwatch just sends me to the back of the line. I get a second chance, but I'm not very smooth the second time around either. I know I can do better, but I don't get a third chance to prove it.

When I head to the next station, I see Calvin showing off his Velcro hands, catching pass after pass. Coach Washington is watching him too, but I can't tell what he's thinking. He's got a great poker face.

Coach Washington glances over and sees me looking at him. He tells me to go to a station where I see a lot of hopeful quarterbacks lining up and throwing balls at different targets. I'm not prepared for this, not at all, but I can't say no. I go over and shuffle my feet nervously on the ground.

I watch the guys in front of me throw short and then incredibly long passes. When I line up I throw a couple of nice short passes, but my long pass is too long. It hits a guy at another station in the back of the helmet.

On the next rotation I meet back up with my first group, but I'm nervous about who may have seen me overthrow the pass.

After four hours, it's finally over.

"How did you do?" I ask Calvin after we each chug a bottle of water.

"I have no idea," Calvin says. "The whole thing felt weird."

As we head back to the locker room, someone touches my arm and says, "Excuse me, young man, do you have a minute?" I find myself face to face with an assistant coach from Branford University.

"I'll catch up to you," I tell Calvin.

"Ignatius Jones, is it?"

I stare at his Branford University polo. I can't seem to say anything, so I just nod.

The guy asks me my stats and then says, "You were impressive out there. Are you interested in Branford?"

Wait, is this really happening?

"Uh—yeah," I stammer. "I've already applied—I sent you guys my game tape . . ."

"Fantastic," he says, before I have a chance

to mention my dad. He hands me his card and tells me he's going to look me up as soon as he gets back to campus, then heads off to talk to another player. For a minute, I'm frozen in place, not sure what this means or how I'm supposed to feel about it. I'd thought UCC was my last chance at a spot on a college football team. But what if I was wrong?

Chapter 16

Mr. Henry meets us at the bus stop when we get back to campus. He drops us off at the dining hall to get some lunch.

"Meet me back at my office in an hour," he says.

Calvin and I gather some food on our trays, but neither of us eat much. We're both nervous about what will happen next. I'm also nervous about what happened at the end of the camp— what the coach from Branford said.

I haven't told Calvin about it, and I'm guessing Calvin is too worried about what UCC thought of us to even consider the

Branford coach. Besides, I'm not even sure if anyone there will actually contact me.

We throw away our half-eaten food and slowly walk across the campus. We're still fifteen minutes early when we get back to the athletic building, so we walk down to the football field and look at it through a closed metal gate.

"Do you picture yourself down there?" I ask Calvin.

He's quiet a moment and stares down at the green field.

"Yeah," he says. "I really do."

I'm not sure what I picture for next year, but for now it's out of my hands, so I try not to think about it.

I look at my phone again. I realize it's time to meet Mr. Henry, and I don't want us to be late.

We head up to the third floor. Kasey meets us there, takes us to a conference room, and tells us Mr. Henry is still in a meeting. I can't tell if she knows anything. Maybe we won't get offers, or maybe she's just already really good at this part of working with prospective athletes. She leaves Calvin and me in the room and closes the door.

"I feel like I can't breathe," Calvin says, nervously tapping his toes. "What if I don't get an offer and you do?" he asks.

I shake my head. "That's not going to happen," I say. "I messed up the three-cone drill *and* my throwing. They seemed more interested in you than me anyway."

For what feels like an hour, we wait in that room. Calvin starts pacing, and I can't help but stare at him as he walks around the room. I can't tell if it's his pacing or my own anxiety, but something is sitting in the pit of my stomach, making me feel sick.

Finally, Mr. Henry comes in. Coach Washington isn't with him, and I take that as a bad sign.

"Calvin," he says. "Please follow me."

I don't know what this means, but after sitting in that room for nearly another thirty minutes, I'm convinced they've decided to take Calvin and not me.

Kasey finally appears.

"Do you know what's going on?" I ask.

"Follow me," she says.

When I get to Coach Washington's office he's sitting behind a desk, and Mr. Henry is sitting in one of the chairs in front of it, but Calvin is gone.

"Sit down," Coach Washington says.

I sit next to Mr. Henry and do my best to look Coach Washington in the eye.

"We're willing to take a big risk on you," he says. "I want you to work with a couple of our coaches and train to be a backup quarterback for the Titans."

I'm stunned. "I haven't played quarterback before, sir," I manage to get out.

"You're fast, and you have good instincts and a strong arm," he says. "I think you have what it takes. We can't give you a full ride, but we can offer you a partial scholarship that often offsets what financial aid doesn't cover."

"Umm, thank you." The words stumble out of my mouth. They don't sound sure or strong. I stand up, extend my hand, and correct myself: "Thank you, this is a great offer."

"A verbal offer," Mr. Henry says. "We'll get the paperwork in order and you'll be able to review it before signing day."

I can't help it—I have to ask. I need to know. "What about Calvin?"

He nods and smiles. "You two push each other. We'd like to pair you out there. Now keep up with your school work, get your application and financial aid paperwork in to us as soon as you can, and we look forward to hearing from you on signing day!"

Chapter 17

As I gather up my things from Shawntrell's room, I get a phone call from the head coach at Branford University. Bob Lewis is his name. He was an assistant coach when my dad played at Branford. He asks me if I'd be willing to meet with him the next day.

"I'm flying back to Oahu tonight," I tell him, and I'm honest with him. "UCC paid for me to come here. They gave me a verbal offer today."

"What if we got you a new ticket home on Monday?" Coach Lewis asks. "We could show you around campus, give you a chance to meet the team, show you pictures of your dad from his time here. Your father was a good guy. We called him Leo the Lion. I'm sorry he's gone."

"Me too," I tell him.

I'm quiet for a moment and then I remember Calvin.

"I'm traveling with a friend," I say. "We came here together. His name is Calvin Gibson. He's an awesome wide receiver. He was at the camp with me. I know he'd love to see Branford too."

There is a long pause.

"We only have one position open on the team," Coach says. "We're looking for a running back. The kid we had our eye on has really disappointed us. He hasn't gotten his grades up. And my assistant coach saw you today and was impressed. I can send a driver to pick you up and bring you over to our school tonight. We're just two hours up the coast."

I take a deep breath. "I really can't just abandon my friend. He's kind of like my brother. I live with his family right now."

"Then we want him to come too," Coach Lewis says, surprising me. "Send me your information, and we'll arrange for you both to get home in time for school on Tuesday."

***

I finish packing and head across the hall. When I knock, Legs answers the door. He scowls and tells me Calvin is taking a shower.

"You don't have to worry about me," I say. "Coach Washington doesn't want me as a running back. He wants me as a backup quarterback."

Legs seems to relax. "He's a smart guy," he says.

Calvin comes down the hall.

"Are you ready?" I ask.

"I still have to pack a couple of things," he says. "But we still have a few hours before Kasey takes us to the airport."

"Go ahead and finish packing and then let's get something to eat," I tell him. "I still have twenty bucks on my card."

In the cafeteria, I tell him about the phone call from Coach Lewis.

"But you've already got an offer here," he says.

"I know," I say. "I just want to go visit the school. Coach Lewis coached my dad."

"Then let's go." Calvin nods. "We'll see the campus, and talk to Coach Lewis. I'm sure he'll have some great stories for you about your dad. But," Calvin gives me a serious look, "I don't want to walk away from UCC. They made us a good offer here. I told them it would be an honor to play for the Titans. I meant that. You and me. Together. Here. This is everything we hoped for."

"Yeah," I say as my phone buzzes with an incoming text. I glance down to read the message.

The driver who will take us to Branford is on his way.

Chapter 18

I lie. I call Kasey from our car and tell her that we have a ride to the airport.

Calvin takes the phone from me and speaks to her. "Thank you for everything. I mean it. It was a great visit, and I can't wait to come back next year."

He's beaming when he hangs up the phone.

"Laying it on kind of thick, aren't you?" I say, smiling at Calvin. "They've already made you an offer. You don't need to keep impressing them."

"Just trying to get on their good side now," Calvin says. "Don't want to start off the season next year on the wrong foot."

We drive along the coast. The sun sets over the ocean.

"Oahu is out there somewhere," I say.

"I'm going to miss it," Calvin says. "My mom thinks next summer she'll get transferred to San Diego, which means they'd move back to the mainland and it would be easier for my parents to come to our games."

I realize that if that happens, I'd no longer have a home in Oahu. I've lived there longer than any other place. It's been my only real home. My dad's ashes were spread there in the bay. Regent High is there. Coach Kainoa is there.

I watch the sun sink into the sea.

We drive up the rest of the coast in the dark and arrive at Branford a little after ten. Even at night, the campus looks amazing—just like I remember it. The buildings are all lit up—glowing against the foothills that rise up behind the campus. A couple of students are walking out of the library as we pass, talking and laughing. I can't help but smile to myself.

Our driver takes us to the athletic office where the assistant coach I talked to at the last-chance camp meets us and takes us to a hotel he booked for us.

"Wait until to you see the place in the morning," I tell Calvin as we open the door to our room. "It's a huge campus. And the stadium . . ."

"I'm so tired," Calvin says, flopping down on one of the beds and turning on the TV.

I don't feel tired, not at all. I'm excited, but Calvin falls asleep.

Chapter
19

The next day, we walk around campus. I point
to the foothills and tell Calvin how my dad
and his teammates used to run them to get in
shape. I tell him a story my dad told me about
how one time, while they were running, one
of the guys got bitten by a rattlesnake, and
they had to carry him all the way down to the
nearest road and wave down help.

"Was the guy okay?" Calvin asks.

"My dad said he played the next Saturday
and swore the venom gave him a boost."

Calvin seems to be only half-listening to
me. He keeps checking his phone and sending

texts. "Coach Kainoa is freaking out that we both got a verbal offer at UCC. He wants to take us out to celebrate. A nice dinner at that restaurant right on the beach, he said. I told him we could go next Saturday."

"Yeah," I say. "That would be fun."

We make our way to the football stadium. Coach Lewis meets us outside the gate and takes us inside.

We head down to the locker rooms and he shows us some pictures of my dad. They even mounted one on the wall. Beneath his picture, in bronze are the words: "It isn't over until the clock says zero."

"He always said that," I tell Coach Lewis. "All the time."

"He never gave up," Coach Lewis said.

"No, he didn't," I agree.

The team is already out on the field to practice, and Coach brings us down there to watch. I'm impressed with the drills he has them run and with how focused each player seems to be.

Unlike at UCC, we don't get called

out on the field to do anything. We're just spectators. It feels good to watch the team work without the added pressure of having to play alongside them.

"Can you imagine being out there?" I ask.

"You will be when we play Branford the next four years," Calvin says. He's looking down at his phone again. It makes me angry. He isn't watching the team, and I know he isn't making a good impression.

"You don't have to be here," I snap.

He looks up at me. "No, *we* don't. We accepted verbal offers at UCC. I don't even know what we're doing here."

I falter. I don't know why, but I can't bring myself to tell Calvin the full truth. So I settle with most of the truth. "I just wanted to see the campus again," I say. "I wanted a chance to talk to Coach Lewis. I wanted to pay some respect to my dad."

"I'm sorry," Calvin sighs, sliding his phone into his back pocket. "You're right." He looks down at the field, and I can tell he really means it.

After a short pause Calvin asks me, "Did you ever get to see any footage of your dad's games?"

"A little," I say.

"You should ask someone if they have more tapes."

I nod at this.

"I want to see him play," Calvin says. "I want to see if you play like him."

Chapter 20

After practice, Coach Lewis sends Calvin on a tour with an assistant coach and takes me into his office.

I ask him if they have any game tapes from when my dad played, and he tells me he'll have some copies made and sent to me.

"Thank you," I say. "I can't wait to watch them. I haven't seen much from when my dad was playing here."

Coach Lewis nods at this and smiles.

"Now let's talk about you," he says.

And we talk. Not only about my season with the Warriors, but also about what I want to study, what I want to do after college. I tell him I'd like to have a career in medicine.

We talk for almost an hour. I feel comfortable sitting in that office. I feel like I'm home.

***

We have lunch with some of the team. When they find out who my dad is, one of the guys tells me that Coach Lewis has talked about him before.

"He's told us we should all play tough. 'Play like Leo Jones,' he tells us. 'Play with the Lion's heart.' 'It isn't over until the clock says zero.'"

I nod at this. I feel like a part of my dad lives on in this place. It's not just his picture on the wall, but his spirit. These guys all seem like hard workers who put their whole hearts into what they're doing. I can tell they respect each other as teammates and have each other's backs. And the vibe I get from them is friendly, like I'm already one of them.

After lunch, Calvin and I head to the airport. It was a short trip, but we've toured the campus, saw my dad's pictures, and I got to talk with Coach Lewis. It was an incredible twenty-four hours. I'm glad we came.

As we walk to our departure gate at the airport, Calvin is quiet.

"What did you think?" I ask.

"It was a nice school," he says. "But they're not interested in me."

"They didn't give me an offer either," I say.

"What would you do if they did?" he asks.

"I don't know," I say, but I do know. I'd go to Branford. I'd play on the same field and sit in some of the same classrooms as my dad did. In a way, it would give me some time with my dad, but I don't know how to explain this to Calvin.

"I'd choose being on the same team with you over being rivals," Calvin says.

I wish Branford would have shown some interest in Calvin. Everything would be perfect then. I know I could convince him to go if he was given an offer, but I don't even know if *I'll* even get one.

This time, our plane leaves on time, and we are back in Oahu at dawn.

Chapter 21

Mrs. Gibson doesn't let us skip another day of school. She gives us time to take a shower and get dressed, but then we have to go.

Calvin puts on his new UCC T-shirt. "Wear yours," he says.

"We'll look dumb wearing the same shirt," I respond.

"Nah," he says. "We'll look like twins."

I laugh at this.

"Seriously," he says. "Wear yours too. We made it!"

But I don't want to wear the shirt, not until I hear back from Branford. There's still a chance I could get an offer. So I put on the UCC shirt and then purposely spill a glass of milk all over it so that I have to change.

At school, our teammates come up to us and slap us on the back. Louie wants to hear all about our trip. "You guys are in!" he says. "You put Regent High on the map."

Ty tells us he's heard that Rain Bok might not get signed anywhere because his grades are so bad.

"Do you know if Branford was looking at him?" I ask.

"They were, but now they aren't," Ty says.

That explains the assistant coach's comment about a top prospect who'd turned out to be a disappointment.

I don't mention Branford to anyone. I didn't even get a verbal offer, so I don't see the point.

At lunch Coach Kainoa comes and finds us. "Wow," he says, approaching our table. He's grinning. "I knew you could do it."

He sits down with us and asks us all about the last-chance camp and the offer they made.

"Quarterback?" he says to me. "Really?"

"Backup," I say. "But if I'm not good, they'd move me back to running back, wouldn't they?"

"I don't know," he says. "Maybe." He looks a little concerned.

"What are you thinking?" I ask

"It just seems so strange that he thinks you should be a quarterback when you're a runner through and through. It's what you do."

"Iggy's also got a great arm," Calvin says. "And he has good instincts."

"Yes, that's true," Coach says, still hesitant. "And Washington is an incredible coach. He knows what he's doing . . . but you've got to want this too, Iggy," he says to me.

"I want to play college football," I say.

"But do you want to play backup quarterback?"

"We'd be out there together," Calvin says.

Coach doesn't look at Calvin—he looks at me. "This is a great offer," he says. "But don't burn any bridges yet. Other doors may still open for you."

"But he already told UCC he'd go there," Calvin says, sounding confused and maybe a little hurt that Coach is reacting this way.

"You boys haven't signed anything yet," Coach reminds us. "And that goes both ways. Keep your grades up and stay out of trouble. Nothing is in ink."

Chapter 22

On Saturday we drive to the restaurant to meet Coach. Mr. and Mrs. Gibson have been invited too but are driving separately. Calvin and I figure we'll hang out on the beach for a little bit after the meal. I'm looking forward to getting back in the water after such a stressful week.

As we get out of our car, my phone rings. At first I think it's my mom, since she always calls on Saturdays, but then I see the area code. The call is coming from California.

"Hello," I answer the phone.

"Iggy," I hear Coach Lewis' voice. "How

have things been?"

"Not bad, thanks . . ." I peel away from Calvin and head to the edge of the parking lot, out of his earshot.

"I enjoyed our visit," Coach Lewis says.

"Me too," I say. "It was great to be there again."

"I'm impressed with your transcript, and I've watched your game tape over and over."

I wait. I don't know what he's going to say next.

"We'd like you to come to Branford and I'd like you to be a part of our team. We've been looking for a strong running back."

"Really?" I say. A wave of excitement surges through me, but then I see Calvin walking toward me.

"I would love to play for you," I say.

"Wonderful. Does that mean you accept this verbal offer?" Coach Lewis asks.

"I accepted a verbal offer at UCC," I say, still watching Calvin come closer.

"It isn't in writing," Coach Lewis says. "You make your final decision on signing day."

"Who is it?" Calvin says to me. "Coach wants to head in. We have a reservation."

"Give me a minute," I say to Calvin, but Coach Lewis thinks I'm talking to him.

"I'll give you some time," Coach Lewis says, sounding disappointed.

"I'm sorry," I say. "I was talking to my friend, Calvin. We're supposed to be somewhere."

"Then I'll let you go. But do feel free to take a few days. Think about it. Just know we want you here."

"Thank you," I say and hang up.

"Who was that?" Calvin asks.

"My mom," I say.

He gives me a weird look, but I don't want to talk about it, not yet. I know what I want to do, but I also know that I don't want to lose my best friend.

Chapter 23

We're seated on the restaurant's outdoor patio. It's a perfect day. Mr. Gibson sits next to Coach Kainoa, and they immediately start talking about college football. Mrs. Gibson sits next to her husband and looks at Calvin and me.

"I'm so proud of you two," she says. "I can't wait to watch you both take the field at UCC. It will be a great day."

When she says it, it hits me: if I were to go to UCC I might not ever actually take the field for the Titans. I would only be trained as a backup quarterback, and if I don't do a good job as a quarterback, I'd probably ride the bench for four years.

I know in my heart I'm not a quarterback.

I look at Coach, and I know what I need to do, but I don't know how to tell Calvin.

The waiter takes our orders and Mr. and Mrs. Gibson keep talking about UCC with Coach Kainoa. I turn to look at Calvin.

He smiles at me, still excited about the UCC conversation.

"Listen," I say quietly. "That wasn't my mom on the phone. It was Coach Lewis from Branford."

His smile falters. "They made you an offer."

"Yeah, and I really want to go there," I say.

Calvin just looks at me. He doesn't say a thing.

Then he gets up and leaves the restaurant.

Chapter 24

Calvin's parents and Coach Kainoa go quiet and look at me, worried. They didn't hear what had just happened between Calvin and me.

I can't look any of them in the eye, so I stare at my shoes as I explain about my call with Coach Lewis and that I want to go to Branford.

There's a long pause. I keep looking down, afraid of the angry faces I might see staring back at me.

Then I feel a pair of arms wrap around me. Mrs. Gibson is hugging me.

"Congratulations!" she says. "That's absolutely amazing! Your father would be so proud."

"It's a great school," Mr. Gibson adds. "They are lucky to have you." He claps me on the back.

"I don't want to disappoint you," I tell them. "Or Calvin. I really appreciate all that you've done for me, but this is something that I've always wanted."

"You need to do what's best for you," Coach tells me. I can see he's happy for me—proud that I've been able to find a place where I feel like I belong.

"But what about Calvin?" I ask, looking around at the three of them.

"He just needs to process everything," Mr. Gibson says. "Give him time. He'll understand."

***

We eat dinner without Calvin. After I've thanked Coach and Mr. and Mrs. Gibson one more time, I head out to find Calvin. His car is still in the parking lot, so he can't have gone far.

As I walk up the beach, I listen to the sound of the ocean. Giant waves come crashing to shore. They slam against the sand with a roar just in time for the next swell to rise up. The water sounds angry as it rips down on the sand.

After a little while I can see someone standing in the shallow water along the shore. Even in the twilight, I don't need to get much closer to be sure that it's Calvin. I could recognize his lanky frame anywhere.

I walk up behind him, and as I get closer he looks back at me. His face is still hard.

"Hey," I say. "Look, I know you're upset, but—"

Before I can finish, Calvin turns away from me and dives deeper into the water. He pops up farther away from me.

I yell out, "I don't want this to change anything between us!"

The waves crash around Calvin and he dives down deep to avoid the worst of the impact.

When he pops back up he yells back "You made a commitment to UCC! To me! Why would you go somewhere else?"

Another big swell crashes, and Calvin bobs down low again.

I kick off my shoes and start walking into the water. The tide pulls at me with every step. I can barely see Calvin in the dark water when he resurfaces. I yell back at him, "It's not about that! Look—"

But before I can finish the sentence, a huge wage smashes down on Calvin.

I wait for him to come out of the water again, but it's taking too long.

"Calvin!" I yell. He doesn't respond. I don't know if I don't see him and he isn't responding because he's angry with me . . . or if he's still under water. I start running farther into the water.

"Calvin!" I scream again, and I see his head break free from the surface. He's gasping for air as another wave comes crashing down on top of him.

"**N**o!"

I swim furiously. The salt water stings my eyes, but I keep them wide open, looking for Calvin.

The water swirls so fast around me that I can't see much of anything. Finally I get a glimpse of an arm, thrashing around in the water.

I swim toward it as another wave comes crashing down. Even under the surface I feel it push me down. Still, I keep swimming. I grab Calvin's arm and pull hard as I kick in the direction of the shore. My mouth burns with the taste of the water.

Soon we reach shallow enough water that we can stand. Calvin and I stumble out of the water, salt water still stinging at our eyes.

Calvin leans on me, coughing and choking on the water that he swallowed. Between gasps of air he looks over at me. His eyes are wide with shock and fear.

We both lie down on the sand. "Are you okay?" I ask him between coughs.

"I was all turned around. I couldn't figure out where the surface was." Calvin's breath has calmed, but his eyes are still wide. "I just kept getting pummeled."

I nod and lie there next to my best friend.

After a long pause Calvin props himself up on his elbows and says quietly, "What about UCC? We were a package deal. What if you tell them no, and then they decide not to take me."

"That's not going to happen. They want you," I say, sitting up. "You've completely won them over."

Calvin looks away and nods. I think he forgives me for the choice I've made—and for not being fully honest with him—but that doesn't mean he feels any better. I know *I* don't feel any better.

The sounds of the waves crashing onto the beach echo all around us.

"I don't know what I'll do at UCC without you," Calvin says.

I don't know what I'll do next year without Calvin either.

Chapter 26

On the first Wednesday in February, Calvin and I enter our school gym. We head to a small table surrounded by TV cameras. Calvin's parents and Coach Kainoa stand nearby, smiling supportively.

Calvin and I each take a seat at the table, facing the cameras. There's a piece of a paper and pen in front of each of us.

"Look at the cameras," someone says. "Three, two, one . . ."

We're introduced by a TV anchor from the local news channel.

"I'm here with two young men who came

out of nowhere and are now in the spotlight. Let's meet them and see where they'll be going next year."

He turns to Calvin. "A star wide receiver from Regent High with 40 receptions for 476 yards and 16 touchdowns."

"And hands of Velcro," I say into the microphone.

Calvin laughs at this.

"And who are you signing with, Calvin Gibson?" the reporter asks.

Calvin leans forward and slips on his UCC hat. "UCC, baby!"

He signs the papers and everyone applauds. His mother kisses him on the cheek and his dad hugs him.

"And Ignatius Jones has 310 carries for 2,211 yards and 15 touchdowns. Regent's finest running back in years. Who will you be signing with?"

I look over at Calvin and his parents.

"First, I'd like to thank the Gibson family and my best friend, Calvin. They took me in so I could finish up my time here at Regent

High. They housed me and fed me and they gave me more than just a home—they gave me confidence and stability. I have so much respect for them." With a smile I add, "But I won't feel bad kicking Calvin's butt in the big UCC-Branford game. I'm going to play for Branford University, just like my father." I pull on my Branford hat.

"Now that's interesting," the anchor says. "Two friends heading to rival schools? How do you think that will impact your friendship?"

"Well," Calvin says, "I'm sure we'll cheer each other on when we aren't playing against each other."

"And," I say, "knowing I'll have to play against Calvin will only make me work harder to make sure the Bears beat the Titans."

Calvin smiles at this. "I'm going to make sure the Titans get the Golden State Bell back."

"We look forward to watching you two play," the anchor says.

A journalist from the local paper asks us a few more questions and takes our picture. Then the gym starts to empty out, and it becomes quiet again.

Calvin and I stand there wearing two different hats.

"This isn't over," Calvin says, sticking out his hand.

"Until the clock says zero," I say, grabbing his hand and shaking it.

Check out all
the GRIDIRON Books

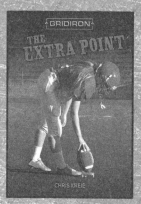

Leave it all on the field!

Check out all the titles in the

bOUnCE Collection

STEP UP YOUR GAME

K. R. Coleman is a writer, teacher, and parent of two boys. Coleman can often be found jotting down ideas in a notebook while watching a hockey or baseball game or while walking along the many trails that encircle Minneapolis. Currently, Coleman teaches at the Loft Literary Center and is working on a young adult novel entitled *Air*.